The SEA SAW

This book is for Bramble Fyra Taylor – TP

SIMON & SCHUSTER

First published in Great Britain in 2019 by Simon & Schuster UK Ltd
1st Floor, 222 Gray's Inn Road, London WC1X 8HB • A CBS Company
Text and illustrations copyright © 2019 Tom Percival • The right of Tom
Percival to be identified as the author and illustrator of this work has been
asserted by him in accordance with the Copyright, Designs and Patents Act,
1988 • All rights reserved, including the right of reproduction in whole
or in part in any form • A CIP catalogue record for this book is available
from the British Library upon request • ISBN: 978-1-4711-7244-1
(HB) • ISBN: 978-1-4711-7243-4 (PB) • ISBN: 978-1-4711-7245-8 (eBook)
Printed in China • 10 9 8 7 6 5 4 3 2 1

The author acknowledges and thanks the Rijksmuseum, Amsterdam for
the use of images from their collection in the creation of the illustrations
for this book.

The SEA SAW

Tom Percival

SIMON & SCHUSTER
London New York Sydney Toronto New Delhi

Sofia's bear was old, tatty and *very* well loved.

It had belonged to Sofia's grandfather, then to her mother and from the day Sofia was born, the bear had kept her company, too.

He was less like a toy and more like a friend.

Sofia and her bear
enjoyed picnics in the park,

long walks through the woods

and, one day, they even went to the seaside.

It was a very long journey: Sofia and her father
had to catch a train, a boat and then *finally* a bus.

But it was worth it . . .

. . . the beach was amazing!

Sofia even took off her bear's scarf
so they could splash in the waves.

Her father bought fish and chips
and they all had ice cream for pudding.

It really was the most *perfect* day.

Until the storm clouds rolled in . . .

Thunder clapped and lightning flashed.

Raindrops pounded down onto the sand as they packed everything up and rushed for the last bus home.

They were in such a hurry that neither of them
noticed a bag fall open and Sofia's bear tumble out.

After the storm had blown over,
the bear sat alone on the wide, empty beach.

And nobody saw, but the Sea.

After a while, a seagull flew down and pecked curiously at the bear.

The Sea saw this and did *not* like it one little bit.

The Sea knew how sad the girl would be to have lost her bear,
and so it decided to help.

As it took hold of the battered bear,
it almost seemed to whisper, *'I will take you home . . .'*

Of course, when Sofia realised that her bear was missing she was terribly upset.

She looked *everywhere* . . .

but he was *nowhere* to be seen.

Her father telephoned the bus company and the train company *and* the boat company – but nobody had found a tatty old bear.

As soon as they could, they returned to the beach, but there was no bear there.

Sofia's father gave her other toys, to try and replace the bear she had lost, but *none* of them were right.

None of them had belonged to her mother.

All that Sofia had left now was the bear's small scarf.

She snipped a piece off, placed it in her locket for safekeeping and tried to carry on as best she could.

But it was just *so* hard.

Now, it's incredibly difficult to return something
when you have no idea who the owner is, or where they live.

But even so, the Sea tried . . .

It washed the bear along through the water,
helped by shoals of shimmering fish,
a whale, a dolphin, and even an octopus.

The bear hitched a lift
on a boat . . .

and he was carried along by a seal.

The Sea always found a way to guide
the bear through the water.

But it was not an easy journey.

When the wind grew cross,
whipping the water into towering waves,
the Sea carried the bear to safety.

When the waters
grew too cold, the Sea
would wash the bear
onto land . . .

and then with spring,

the journey
would begin again.

The Sea became concerned – it was all taking so long!

It carried the bear to every beach and every dock
and every harbour, too – but with no luck.

And so the search went on . . .
beyond the oceans, into lakes and along rivers.

Which was how the bear came to be gently drifting
down a stream one sunny afternoon.

A young girl saw the bear floating in
the shallow waters and went to investigate.

Curious, she picked it up and called out to her grandmother,
to tell her all about this exciting new find.

Slowly, the old lady walked out of the house.
Then she stopped.

She stared silently for a moment,
then rushed forwards to scoop
up the bear.

Sofia hugged her bear close
for the first time in
many, many years.

You see, nothing is ever *truly* lost
if you keep it in your heart.

The next day, they returned to the beach Sofia
had visited all those years ago.

She stood on the warm sand looking far out to sea.
Then she smiled . . .

and the Sea saw.